My Mother's Sari

WRITTEN BY **Sandhya Rao** ILLUSTRATED BY **Nina Sabnani**

NORTHSOUTH
BOOKS
New York / London

My mother's sari.

3 Now make a few
wide pleats in the front.

4 Tuck the pleats
into the slip.

Text copyright © 2006 by Sandhya Rao
Illustrations copyright © 2006 by Nina Sabnani.
First published in India by Tulika Publishers under the title *My Mother's Sari*.
New English edition copyright © 2006 by North-South Books Inc.

First published in the United States, Great Britain, Canada, Australia, and New Zealand in 2006 by
North-South Books Inc., an imprint of NordSüd Verlag AG, Gossau Zürich, Switzerland.
Distributed in the United States by North-South Books Inc., New York.

Library of Congress Cataloging-in-Publication Data is available.
A CIP catalogue record for this book is available from The British Library.

ISBN-13: 978-0-7358-2101-9 / ISBN-10: 0-7358-2101-1 (trade edition)
10 9 8 7 6 5 4 3 2 1

Printed in Belgium

My mother's sari

is long like a train.

It fills

the air with color
when I dance and sing.

I sail down a river

and climb up a rope.

I hide with my friends.

I even wipe my nose.

Then, when I am tired,
it wraps itself around me.

I sleep while it gently swings
beneath a shady tree.

I love my mother's sari . . .

and how it makes me dream.

5 Gather the rest of the sari, take it around the waist and bring to the front.

6 Now take it across the chest and throw the end over the left shoulder.